# Chart Topper

# THE OPPORTUNITY

# Chart Topper

### D. M. PAIGE

darby creek

MINNEAPOLIS

Darby Creek
A division of Lerner Publishing Group, Inc.
241 First Avenue North
Minneapolis, MN 55401 U.S.A.

Website address: www.lernerbooks.com

Cover and interior photographs © Jason Stitt/Dreamstime.com (girl);
© iStockphoto.com/Jordan McCullough (title texture).

Main body text set in Janson Text LT Std 12/17.
Typeface provided by Linotype AG.

The Cataloging-in-Publication Data for *Chart Topper* is on file at the Library
of Congress.
    ISBN: 978-1-4677-1370-2 (LB)
    ISBN: 978-1-4677-1672-7 (EB)

Manufactured in the United States of America
1 – SB – 7/15/13

*In order to succeed, your desire for success
should be greater than your fear of failure.*

—*Bill Cosby*

# PROLOGUE

Dear Ms. Beth Thorne:

Welcome to the Harmon Holt internship program.

You will be spending the summer interning with Bonified Records, one of the most successful music recording companies of all time.

The recording industry is changing rapidly, and the artist is becoming more and more responsible for his or her success. While you have much to learn about the business from the label, they also have much to learn from you as an artist yourself. My team and I had the pleasure of viewing your YouTube videos—your songs and your voice made quite the impression. We would like the opportunity to foster your talent—and to be there at the start of your very promising career.

It may be hard to see it now, but the distance between me and you is hard work and opportunity. I am giving you the opportunity. The rest is up to you.

Good luck,
Harmon Holt

# ONE

I was sitting in the library, checking my e-mail, when it happened. I heard my song. I tried to ignore it. It had to be some kind of coincidence. But then another person started humming, too. And another. And another.

Mrs. Jane, the librarian, was not pleased. She stood up from her desk and frowned over the class. It was study hall. We were all supposed to be researching our last paper of the year for English. But most of us were distracted by e-mails, games, and YouTube.

I clicked my screen back to a search on

themes in *Romeo and Juliet* for my paper. And I prayed for the humming to stop.

"Who's doing that?" she demanded, putting her hands on her hips.

"Ask Beth. It's her song," said Michelle Morris, one of the popular kids. She was captain of our school's cheer squad, the star of every school play and musical, prom queen. . . . Michelle was high school royalty. She smiled a big smile and turned her computer screen to share it with Mrs. Jane and the rest of the class. It was me. My video on YouTube. Me singing one of my songs.

It was my little secret. I would tape the songs that I wrote and put them up. I didn't use my name. I used "Girl with a Guitar." I figured no one from school would ever know. It was fun. It was mine. It seemed like such a good idea until this very second.

I'd managed to stay off of Michelle's radar through most of high school. We were juniors now, and she probably had said maybe five words to me since were little kids. Michelle was a bit of a mean girl. But she usually only picked on girls her own size—girls who held as much clout in the halls of Clinton High as she did. Like her feud with Tamara Kim, her cocaptain on the cheer squad, or her Twitter war with Stephy Jenkins, the girl who beat her for homecoming queen last year.

Looking at the screen, I wondered if maybe she was confusing me with one of those girls. I looked like a totally different person on-screen. Sure, I had the same brown hair, cropped short like Rihanna's was a few years back, and the same brown eyes and skin. But I was different. Singing at the top of my voice, beaming out at the web camera. I was never like that at school. I was quiet. Shy even. My classmates were leaning in like they were surprised to see this other me too.

Mrs. Jane, thankfully, turned off the screen. "Ms. Thorne is very talented, but now is not the time or the place."

The class laughed. I just wasn't sure if it was with or at me. I looked for Mercedes's reaction. She was my BFF, and she was sitting in the front row of computers. But she was facing forward, away from me.

The bell rang, and everyone began filing out of the library. Mercedes sat down beside me after everyone else moved on. Her backpack dropped in a heap beside me. I read the face that I knew almost as well as my own. She was half-excited, half-mad.

Excited because she liked what she heard, and mad because she hadn't heard it before everyone else.

"I'm never going to live this down, am I?" I sighed.

"I hope not," she said.

I looked up, surprised.

"Your song was so good. I knew you sang, but you took it to a whole other level. When did you get so good, and how could you not let me know? How could you hide that? Why didn't you tell us?" Mercedes said in a rush.

I shrugged. "I thought no one would ever see it."

"But you put it on the Internet! Wasn't that the point?"

She had a point. Maybe I did want people to see. But not like this.

"You really think it was good?" I asked again, needing to know. If anyone in the world would be honest with me, it would be Mercedes.

Mercedes looked me directly in the eye, like she was making a point of being serious. She said her words slowly, like she really wanted me to understand.

"I would think it was good even if you weren't my girl."

Then she paused and bit her lip. "Did you see Michelle's face? She was totally hating on you."

"So . . ."

"She's jealous, because you sing better than her."

"I don't know about that," I said. But I found myself smiling. Michelle had starred in every school musical from *The Wiz* to *Les Miserables*. Her voice was way prettier than her personality.

"I do. Do you know the difference between you and Michelle?"

"Everything."

"She thinks she's more talented than she actually is, and you're the exact opposite. You don't have a clue how good you are."

I opened my mouth to protest. But Mercedes was already back up on her feet. She gave me a quick hug and skipped out of the library.

I started to gather my backpack and books, but then I noticed I had new e-mail from an address I'd never seen before.

It was a request for a video chat.

# TWO

A video chat window popped up on screen. There was a guy who looked like a male model. He was so tall, dark, and handsome that he looked like he should be on the cover of a magazine or something, not talking to me on my tiny computer screen. He was holding a piece of blue paper.

"Hi, Beth. I'm James, one of Harmon Holt's assistants. You'll be getting a copy of this in the mail. But Harmon wanted you to hear about it right away."

Harmon Holt? *The* Harmon Holt. The multibillion-dollar mogul behind all kinds of media and business ventures. Why would he—or his really, really hot assistant—be video messaging me? I looked around. Was this some kind of joke? Maybe Michelle orchestrated it. She didn't like me. But this seemed like too much even for her.

The guy on-screen began to read in a deep voice, "'Dear Ms. Thorne, Welcome to the Harmon Holt internship program.

"'You will be spending the summer interning with Bonified Records, one of the most successful music recording companies of all time. . . . My team and I had the pleasure of viewing your YouTube videos—your songs and your voice made quite the impression. We would like the opportunity to foster your talent and to be there at the start of your very promising career.' And it's signed, 'Good luck, Harmon Holt.'"

The cute guy looked up from the letter and looked right into the camera. "I see you accept. I'll see you next week in New York."

The screen went blank. I sat back in my chair.

New York. Bonified Records! There no way this was true. It was one of those crazy

Internet scams where they follow up and ask you to send money to Nigerian princes or something. It wasn't my real life.

But five seconds later, Mrs. Jane looked at me and said, "Oh, good you're still here. The guidance counselor wants to see you. Don't worry it's not a bad thing."

I followed her out. This couldn't be real, could it?

# THREE

"I don't understand. There are tons of kids who are in the music program. Why me and not them?" I asked as I sat in front of Ms. Hamilton's desk in her office.

Clinton High was known for its arts programs, but I was there for its academics. I was a good student. But I wasn't one of those kids that it came easily to. I had to study hard for every single A. But it was worth it. All the work was paying off, and I was on track to get into a good state school. The music thing was something I did on my own time. I wasn't good in front of crowds, and the musical-theater kids were really good at being in front of people. So I wasn't one of them. And no matter what Mercedes said about Michelle, I wasn't really a threat to her because I would never, ever get on stage at our school.

Mrs. Hamilton was super excited for me. She clapped her hands together and handed me the blue letter. A copy of the same one I had seen on the video.

"Your video came to the attention of Mr. Holt. He feels like you are the perfect candidate."

"How?"

"Mr. Holt works in mysterious ways. It's a tremendous opportunity, Beth. Remember how we talked about having a well-rounded resume for college applications? This internship, your music would actually be the perfect thing to make you that much more attractive to colleges. This is a win-win for you."

I left the office, holding the letter tight in my hands. I stuffed it into my notebook and carried it around with me all day, reading it and re-reading it to make sure that it was actually real.

# FOUR

Asking my mom if I could spend the summer in New York on my own was like asking her if I could go to the moon.

But I had to ask.

Mom was still wearing her nurse's scrubs. She looked tired from pulling the late shift. She sat down in a chair at our kitchen table.

She took off her ugly white nurse's shoes. They looked comfortable, but Mom said that after ten hours nothing was comfortable. I heated up the dinner I'd made for her in the microwave and put it in front of her.

Mom pushed the chicken around on her plate before taking a bite. It wasn't that she didn't like my cooking. It was that she wasn't a fan of healthy food. Mom had been on a low-salt, low-sugar diet since she found out she was prediabetic last year.

"It tastes better than it looks. I promise."

She took a bite. And finally broke into a smile.

"Not bad, but not as good as my chocolate cake."

Chocolate cake had been off the menu at our house for over a year now. I ate whatever Mom ate, or didn't. We had both lost five pounds since she started the diet. Only I didn't really need to. Unlike my mom, who was all curves, I didn't have any.

"Mom—something happened at school today."

"I know. I already got a call from your counselor."

"I want to go."

"Of course you want to go. But that doesn't mean that it's a good idea. I see girls your age in the ER every night."

"Mom, I know, but I'll be careful. I'll just go to my internship and back to the dorm. My counselor says it will increase my chances for a scholarship."

"I thought music was just a hobby?" She said it like it was an order, not a question. And it kind of was.

"It is."

It hurt to call it that, but Mom was right. I had to be realistic. My mom could sing, too. Her voice might even be better than mine. But she only sang in church and in the shower.

"I don't want you getting any big ideas in your head, B. The plan is college. I've seen way too many girls take detours with big dreams and small ones."

I nodded. Mom wanted me to go to school and study something serious like law or medicine. Something that she was sure I could get a job in and succeed. She didn't want me to get sidetracked. And I didn't want me to get sidetracked either. But I wasn't dropping out of school to sing in nightclubs. I was going to spend the summer at a major record label, learning the business and beefing up my resume. If anything, it would help Mom's realistic dreams for me.

"But having something like this on my college application, it might make a difference. There will be an RA on the hall I'm staying in in the dorm. And I'll have my phone. Mom, please."

"I'll think about it."

It wasn't a no. And, knowing Mom, it was probably as close to yes as she could get. I gave her a hug.

\*\*\*

A few minutes later, I picked up the phone to call Mercedes. I held the phone away from my ear because she was screaming so loud.

# FIVE

When I got to school, everyone had heard about it. Or, rather, Mercedes had told everyone.

"I heard she got a record deal in New York," someone said as I rounded the corner to algebra.

"I heard it was L.A. and that she's dropping out of school to do it," someone else said as I slammed the door of my locker before English.

I wasn't good at getting a lot of attention. But by sixth period I'd had like ten people congratulate me. Most of them looked beyond surprised that I would have anything to do with the music business. The rest had seen my video.

Mercedes was enjoying it a lot more than I was.

"You're already a star," Mercedes said, linking her arm through mine and sounding way more sure than I felt.

"It's just for college applications. I am not going to be a star. I'm going to be getting coffee and making copies for people who make stars."

"Keep telling yourself that," Mercedes said, clearly not believing me.

In English class, Michelle was playing my song again. Or, rather, singing. She definitely was making fun of me.

I opened my notebook and looked at the letter again. I didn't say anything. It was enough to know I was going.

# SIX

A week later, an SUV picked me up from the airport after my very first flight. There had been some turbulence, and I had held onto my seat's armrest for dear life while the other passengers continued to drink their beverages and ignored the seat belt warning light. I was shakier now as the SUV drove into the city and the buildings I'd seen my whole life on TV cropped up beside the car. I was in New York City!

The TV screen behind the driver's seat suddenly came to life. Harmon Holt's assistant's pretty face filled the screen. I jumped up in my seat.

The driver announced a little too late that the car was equipped with videoconferencing. And that I had a call.

"Hello, Beth. James here. I help Mr. Holt with everything," Harmon's assistant explained as I recovered from the surprise of the TV screen talking to me.

"Hi, James," I said, waving at the screen. Then I put my hand down, feeling a little silly about the wave.

"I'm sorry I couldn't be there. I'm in Beijing with Mr. Holt on urgent business. But you have all my contact info, and if you have any problems at all, please don't hesitate to contact us. I'll e-mail you all my information."

"Thanks," I said as James disappeared and the screen went back to black.

I took a water from the SUV's minibar and took a massive gulp. I guessed this was how people in Harmon Holt's world lived. I reminded myself not to get used to it. I was just visiting.

A few minutes later, I was in my home for the next three months: the tenth floor of NYU's dorms. The dorms were mostly full of college students. But two floors were reserved for high school kids who had internships in the city. There were two beds and two desks. Someone had already been there. There was an open suitcase and a pink bedspread on the bed closest to the window. I took the other bed and began unpacking my stuff.

A guy who looked a few years older than me knocked on my door.

"You must be Beth. I'm Tom. I'll be your summer resident adviser. Anything I can help with?"

I shook my head. "No, thanks."

I was surprised that my resident advisor was a boy. Mom would not be thrilled. The dorm and the floor were coed.

"Bathrooms are down the hall. They're cleaned daily, but I'd still recommend shower shoes. We'll have a floor meeting tonight and once a week. Everyone has dorm duties so that we can get to know each other. I know that everyone's doing their own thing this summer, but I want you to think of this place as your home base. The other kids here are going out there every day to their internships, too, so they actually might be the best ones to talk to about what it's like to be an intern."

"Sounds good. Thanks."

He nodded and shut the door behind him.

I sank down on my bed. I'd make it up later. Now I just needed a moment of peace to get used to . . . whatever this was.

A few seconds later, my lock turned and a pretty, dark-haired girl entered.

"Hi, I'm Paloma."

Oh well.

# SEVEN

I wasn't great at making new friends, but Paloma was super friendly. She was from New Mexico, and she was doing an internship at a fashion magazine in the city.

"It's just an internship, but if I do well, I think I'll get to come back next summer. Or maybe I'll try a different magazine. The important thing is that I'm making connections. I want to write. And one day I'll be writing for them or someone like them." She talked fast, so fast that I half-expected her to have to catch her breath when she paused. But she didn't seem to need to breathe. "What about you?"

I was surprised by her confidence. I was pretty sure that I wouldn't get to have the thing that I knew deep down I wanted. I would never be a singer. Except like my mom, in the shower and at church. But that didn't mean I couldn't enjoy the summer.

I told her I was working at Bonified in A&R.

"What does A&R stand for, anyway?" she asked, her face lit up with curiosity. As much as she talked, she also liked to listen.

"Everyone thinks it stands for artists and recording—or artists and records—but it's artists and repertoire, which a fancy way of saying that A&R handles everything that an artist does, from publishing rights to recording. Everything that the label does for the artist from the second they sign to the second they get released." I hadn't known what A&R stood for until after I got Harmon Holt's blue letter and looked it up.

"Cool," Paloma said. "So do you want to be a big-time music exec or something?"

I shrugged. "I sing, a little."

"Like what kind of stuff? Hip-hop, R&B, pop?"

"Like R&B, I guess."

I wrote about everything. Boys I liked at school who didn't know I was alive. Girls who annoyed me like Michelle. Friends like Mercedes who made life at Clinton bearable.

"Cool, you're going to rule the music world and I'm going to rule fashion."

She pulled a box that smelled like sugar out of her bag.

"My mom makes the best sugar cookies."

I reached out and took my first bite of sugar in ages. I looked out the window, which faced a little New York park. Could life get any sweeter?

# EIGHT

Bonified took up an entire office building. It was in the middle of downtown New York, overlooking the Hudson River. The security guard downstairs sent me up to the top floor, where J. T. Lane, CEO of Bonified, ruled over his empire.

The building was thirty stories high. If I wasn't nervous before, I was after the elevator ride, which took half the length of a song from one of the label's major artists: Pippa. Pippa was just a year older than me, and she already had two hit albums. And she was already one of those stars that just went by one name, like Beyoncé or Mariah. Her music was the kind of stuff that got stuck in your head even if you didn't want it there. And she was known for elaborate stage shows and costumes, like Gaga and Nicki Minaj. Lately, she'd been sporting blue hair—which somehow looked amazing on her. Her skin tone was the same honeyed brown as mine. But I wouldn't caught dead in blue hair. Of course, I wasn't known for taking fashion risks. Right now, I felt super uncomfortable, having given up my usual uniform of jeans and a T-shirt for a pleated skirt and a blouse that my mom had bought for me so I would look presentable.

When I stepped out of the elevator there was guy waiting for me next to the receptionist's desk.

"Hi, I'm Malik, J. T.'s assistant."

Malik looked like a younger version of that English rapper I always forgot the name of, Lil' Sean or Dr. Sean or something. He was wearing a striped button-down shirt and dark blue jeans and Converse. I hoped that meant that I was allowed to wear jeans too.

Malik looked young. But not as young as me. I wondered if he'd started out as an intern too.

He shook my hand and led me through the automatic frosted-glass double doors and into the Bonified offices.

I was expecting some kind of supermodern offices, but instead it looked like a fancy hotel with wingback chairs and French furniture and silvery brocade-y wallpaper. But up close, you could see the wallpaper had little tiny record players all over it. And the portraits that lined the wall were of the label's biggest stars.

"Not what you were expecting, huh?" Malik offered. I nodded. "The first time I got here, I thought I was walking into a museum. But J. T. says that he likes the classic stuff, because one day what he's making will be considered masterpieces, too."

I almost laughed. Pippa's latest single was called "Papercut My Heart." Catchy, but I wasn't sure I'd call it a masterpiece. I wondered if you had to have a huge ego to work in this business. Malik didn't seem to. But he was still an assistant.

He pushed into the heavy walnut door that led to J. T.'s office. J. T. sat behind his desk, poring over something on his iPad.

J. T. Lane looked exactly like what I thought a music producer would look like. He looked beyond cool. And expensive. Everything had a label I recognized—Fendi glasses, Polo shirt. His own one-of-a-kind Nike sneakers peeked out from under the heavy wood desk.

"J. T., this is our new intern. The one that Harmon sent. Beth, this is J. T."

He started speaking even before I could say hi.

"Usually we don't take high school kids. They lack the maturity to handle what we do here. Their feelings get hurt. I am not a babysitter."

I almost laughed. I was a really old sixteen. I'd been taking care of myself and my mom for as long as I could remember.

"So there will be ground rules to make this work."

I nodded.

"Consider yourself an invisible person.

Only speak when spoken to. I say jump . . ." He paused.

"I say, 'How high?'" I guessed.

"Wrong. Trick question. Remember the first rule—"

"Only speak when spoken to," I said. Technically, he *had* spoken to me, but I wasn't going to point that out.

"I think she's got it," Malik jumped in, in a tone that seemed to say, "Cool, it J. T., she's a kid."

J. T. looked up, surprised, like Malik didn't unusually interrupt him. He almost looked embarrassed. Almost.

"Malik will get you settled," he said and became interested in his iPad. It looked like the digital issue of *Rolling Stone*. Pippa was on the cover. She was the label's hottest artist right now.

I wanted to tell him that talking too much had never been a problem for me. But that would require speaking again.

"So Harmon says you're the next Beyoncé or something," he said, looking me up and down as if trying to see what Harmon was talking about.

"I don't know about that."

"I don't know about that either, and I don't want to know until after the internship is over. So keep the demo CD in your pocket until the summer is over."

"I wasn't going to try to hand you anything," I said honestly.

"Then maybe you don't belong in this business."

"But you just said—"

"I will say no, but you should always, always be trying."

I walked away feeling more confused than ever.

# NINE

Malik gave me the grand tour. Every floor had a purpose. Publicity, social media, accounting. He told me I was lucky because I'd spend most of my time in with J. T.

The label was its own universe. It had its own cafeteria and coffee shop and juice bar. It actually had its own in-house recording studio. He saved that for last.

"How do you feel about Pippa?" he asked as he pushed open the door to the studio's control room.

The recording light was on outside the door to the sound booth. He put his finger to his lips, so I couldn't respond that I had every single song. And that I'd even covered a few and put them up on YouTube.

Through the glass of the recording studio, I could see Pippa. *The* Pippa. But Pippa was in the middle of a tantrum.

I have never thrown a tantrum in my life. And I'd never seen anyone over the age of three throw one. But Pippa was throwing a tantrum. Her pretty face was red. Her arms were flailing. And she literally was stomping her six-inch heels.

She stopped suddenly and flashed me a big smile as Malik opened the door to the sound booth. She straightened up to her full height and towered even further over me.

"Do you know who you are?" the words spilled out of my mouth. The last thing I wanted to be was to be the super fangirl.

Pippa laughed. "I do. Do you know who you are?"

I was hoping that when I finally met her I would play it cool, like it was no big deal. But I totally failed.

I paused a couple of seconds, but she said nothing.

Pippa actually wanted to know who I was.

"Me, I'm nobody—I mean, I'm Beth." I looked up at her pretty face. She was so calm now, and I was the complete opposite. She was the first famous person I'd ever met.

"Nice to meet you, not-nobody. No one on my team is a nobody."

# TEN

J. T. announced his presence by growling, "Blair, don't disturb the talent."

"Beth's not disturbing me, J. T. Don't be so rude." She turned back to me, but she spoke louder for J. T.'s benefit. "He thinks that being a jerk gives him power. I think it's because he was some super shy kid who never talked, and now he's trying to make up for it."

She could have been describing me. Only I hadn't made up for my shyness. I glanced at J. T., who was smiling, but I knew he was seething underneath. I couldn't see another, younger

J. T. who was nerdy or shy. I figured he was born like this—cocky and sure of everything. Right now he was probably wishing that he had never hired me.

Malik put his hand on my shoulder, reminding me that it was time to go. I tried to snap out of fan mode. I waved to Pippa, who smiled at me and let Malik push me back out the door.

"Was I as bad as I think I was?" I asked.

He laughed. "The first time I met Drake, I actually quoted one of his rhymes to him."

"What did he say?" I asked, feeling a little better already. Malik had a way of putting me at ease even though I barely knew him.

"He did the same thing Pippa did. He laughed and smiled. Pippa's used to people turning to mush around her. It's okay."

I wondered what it would be like to have people get tripped up just meeting me. I couldn't imagine it.

"Come on, I'll show you the gym," he said before taking off down the hall.

"You have your own gym?" I asked, wondering if this place could get any more fabulous.

# ELEVEN

The next day I made a point of getting to work ten minutes early. I didn't want to be late.

Malik walked me through my responsibilities. I would follow him through the day as he followed J. T.

"The rest we'll make up as we go along."

J. T. had a breakfast meeting with his VP of social media. Malik took notes on his tablet.

I was there to listen and to go fetch anything that J. T. wanted.

The social media guy looked like he wasn't much older than us, but it was like he was speaking a whole other language. I knew about Twitter and YouTube and Facebook, but he talked about them like they weren't just for fun. They were another way to measure and predict how an artist's album would do. Pippa had millions of followers, and they were active. J. T. looked down at the numbers and seemed more than pleased. It was boring and fascinating all at once.

Malik got a text from the recording studio and whispered to me, "Head down to the studio and get her whatever she wants."

"Get *who* whatever she wants?" I asked.

"Pippa," he said it like it was no big deal.

"And what do you think she'll want?" I asked, not wanting to see another one of Pippa's tantrums.

"Relax, you'll be fine," he whispered, turning his attention back to J. T.

I tiptoed out of the room, not completely sure. What if she threw a phone at me, or worse?

\*\*\*

When I got to the recording studio, Pippa wasn't

throwing anything. She was sitting calmly on her stool, looking at her sheet music. But her sound engineer, Mike, didn't look happy. He looked almost like he was going to cry.

"What is it? What is she doing?" I asked Mike.

The sound guy shook his head. "Nothing. She won't sing."

"What does she want?"

He shook his head again.

"No clue. She's not talking to me either. Good luck. I'm going to go get a coffee."

He walked out.

I took a deep breath and entered the sound booth.

Apparently there was something worse than Pippa screaming. It was Pippa not talking at all.

She studied me for a beat as if trying to place me.

"I'm Beth. I heard that you might need something."

She didn't answer. She kept staring at me.

"Can I get you anything? Water, coffee, Coco-water—"

She was the poster girl for Coco-water, one of those fancy bottled-water drinks, and whenever she wasn't photographed holding a giant Frappuccino, she was carrying a bottle of Coco-water.

"Can I tell you a secret? I hate Coco-water."

I almost gasped, but I pursed my lips together instead.

She leaned closer to me, whispering again. "And J. T. didn't discover me singing in the subway, either. J. T. doesn't even take the subway. It was a casting call, and I was the lucky girl."

I gasped for real this time. I'd read about Pippa getting discovered with her guitar on the subway. I'd even tacked up an article of her talking about it over my desk back home. I got that she was making money off of the ads— but why not pick something she liked? And the other lie didn't seem worth it. I was a terrible liar myself. I couldn't keep up with stupid fake details like that.

Pippa seemed to read my outrage on my face. "It makes me seem more like a real girl," she quipped.

"Don't you want the fans to know the real you?"

She laughed again. "You really are completely new to all this, aren't you?"

I nodded, feeling self-conscious.

"It's a persona—it sells. I'm a brand, not a person," she rolled on.

"You're more than that. I've been listening to your music. It means a lot to a lot of people."

She shrugged, looking unsure for the first time since I'd met her.

"Can you get Mike back in here? I think I'm ready to sing now."

"Sure."

I raced out, smiling a little. I had talked down my first star. But I felt a little bad, too. It's not like I could pity her, exactly. I mean, she had everything, right?

# TWELVE

No one was using the recording studio. I was supposed to be cleaning up after Pippa left. But my eyes got stuck on the microphone in the center of the recording booth. I couldn't not stand in front of it. It might be the same mic that Beyoncé or Usher or Christina Aguilera sang their first big hit on.

I caught a glimmer of my own reflection in the glass of the sound booth. And something else.

Malik was standing in front of the sound-board. I stopped singing and stepped away from the mic.

"Nice pipes," he said.

"I was just . . ."

"Don't stop on my account." He was smiling.

The spell was broken for me. I couldn't sing in front of him. I couldn't sing in front of anyone. I rushed over to where Pippa had left her water bottle and song sheet and picked them up.

"I know he gave you the whole don't-give-me-your-work thing. He comes on hard. But he's good to his people. I started out an intern too."

I wasn't sure if I believed him about J. T. I thought maybe he was just trying to make me feel better.

"You did amazing with Pippa yesterday. She doesn't usually respond that well to anyone. She went through the whole session without stopping once. Which is kind of a miracle for Pippa."

"Thanks, but I don't think I deserve the credit."

He shrugged.

"I didn't think she'd be so . . ." I searched for the right word.

Malik tried to fill in the blank. "Crazy?"

I shook my head. "Unsatisfied."

# THIRTEEN

"Everyone out!" Pippa's voice filled the room as she screamed into the mic in the recording studio the next day.

I'd been bringing Pippa a glass of regular, non-Coco water, when she suddenly began yelling.

"Everyone out," she repeated.

I stood for a second like a deer in headlights, not sure whether I should deliver the water first.

The sound guy, Mike, gave me a look that said I should save myself. He held the door open for me behind him as he exited.

"Hey, Beth."

She remembered my name. I turned around.

"Stay."

I walked back to her.

"I just wanted to listen to the track on my own," she said quietly. She wanted me to listen to it with her. She sat at the soundboard, and her song filled the little room. I sat down, not really sure what she was doing.

It was just her voice; the instruments would be added back in later. It sounded pure and great and happier than the girl in front of me, who was frowning at the sound of her own voice.

When the song finished, she said, "You were honest with me the other day. I need you to be honest with me again. What do you think, really think, of my song? Because I think it sucks."

"Your voice is so amazing. It sounds even better than it does on your album," I began.

She sighed as if she already knew that about her voice, "Not my voice. The song. And be honest. I can take it."

What could I say? Did I tell her the truth? Malik had praised me for getting Pippa to calm down yesterday, but if I told her the truth, she'd be the opposite of calm.

"I think it's great. But I also thought it was great the first time I heard it three years ago, when Beyoncé sang it."

"It's not the same song."

"It's the same basic melody. But the words are different." *And Beyoncé's were better,* I thought, but I didn't want to add any more fuel to Pippa's fire.

She pushed play again. She clamped her hand over her mouth and then stopped it.

"Oh no, it is pretty close, isn't it? Why didn't anyone tell me? How could J. T. bring this to me?"

This wasn't good. She was going to complain to J. T. He was totally going to fire me.

"I need something new. Something that's all mine."

"Then why don't you write something? About you—the real you."

I got up and left her to think about it.

"Maybe I will," she said when I got to the door.

I don't know why I did it. I couldn't lie to her. It wasn't like I owed her anything. But there was something about the way she looked at me. Like she had all these people around her and a million fans. But she didn't have one person to tell her the truth. So I did.

\*\*\*

When I got back upstairs, I was planning on blurting out the whole encounter to Malik. But he caught me completely off guard with his first question.

"What are you doing after work?" he asked. Was Malik asking me out? He was too old for me. And he was kind of my boss. "Not like that. It's work-related."

"Oh, sure, right. I'd love to. I mean . . . nothing. I'm not doing anything."

# FOURTEEN

"You trust me, right?" Malik asked an hour later as I looked at my cell phone again. I had texted my mom to tell her that I was doing something for work.

We were standing in a little lounge in SoHo called the Living Room. It had a little stage and tons of little couches and tables. It was dimly lit, with candles on each table providing the only light.

Malik seemed to know the hostess and the waitresses. And he had a table reserved right up front near the little stage.

"Are we scouting a new band or something?" I assumed.

"It's open mic night," he explained.

"Do you just come and look for new singers every night?" I knew that part of what Bonified did was discover new artists. It was so cool that part of Malik's job included listening to new music every night.

"No, I want you to get up there and sing."

"You what?"

My stomach dropped.

"That's not going to happen."

"It would be good for you. Every artist needs to hear what his or her work sounds like in the real world. Otherwise you might as well be singing by yourself in your room."

"You don't get it. I'd rather be singing by myself in my room. I have total stage fright. I get dizzy, and I can't speak, let alone sing. I can't."

"What if I do it with you?" he offered.

"You sing, too?"

"No, I'm terrible, but it will make you see how good you are," he said lightly.

"I'll forget all the words. I just can't."

"Okay, okay. I had no idea. You just seem like you'd love this kind of thing."

"Have you met me?"

"Yeah, you stood up to Pippa. I figured this would be a piece of cake."

I laughed. And finally felt my body relax. I turned for the door.

"We're here anyway. Why don't we just listen this time, and next time we can see what you can do."

*Next time?* I looked around. The place was filling up with kids around my age. It looked cool.

"Okay."

I sat back down on one of the tufted chairs. Malik sat across from me, smiling again. The girl on stage was singing her heart out, doing a full-on rendition of an old Rihanna song. She wasn't doing it justice.

Malik ordered food for us, and we chowed down on appetizers while we scored the singers. Malik had a great ear for who was pitchy and who was on key. He also slipped in a few thoughts of his own about the song he'd heard me singing that day. I'd never gotten any feedback on my songs unless I counted the stream of comments on the videos, and all of those came from people who knew me at school.

"I did something stupid today."

Malik raised his eyebrows.

"You know how you said I stood up to Pippa? Well, I did it again. Only this time I think I did something much worse. "

I blushed and then explained what had happened. He listened, and I waited for him to tell me exactly how much trouble I was in.

"There's no way she's actually going to listen to you. She's Pippa. She probably threw about ten tantrums and changed the color of her hair since then. I bet she's forgotten all about it."

He started laughing. I joined in. He was right. There was no way Pippa would throw out a song for me.

# FIFTEEN

When I got there in the morning, a cell phone
whizzed by my ear as I walked into the recording studio, balancing four coffees on a tray. Malik was wrong. Pippa hadn't forgotten. She must
have told J. T. what I'd said about the song.

"I know what I want now, J. T. And it's your
job to give it to me. I'm the artist and the artist is always right," Pippa said, confusing herself
with that motto of the customer always being
right. But now was not the time to correct her.
She was on a roll. She knocked over the music
stand with one of her six-inch heels and looked

59

around for something else to hurl in J. T.'s direction. Pippa looked down at her shoes, but they had way too many straps. Still, she bent over to try to pull one of them off. I gulped down a laugh. And wondered if I should call Malik.

"No!" J. T. said as he stood up from a crouched position. He must have ducked to miss the phone.

This time Pippa was using her tantrum to get something hat she actually wanted.

I smiled and picked up the phone off the floor.

I stopped smiling when I came face-to-face with J. T.

"I want to see you in my office," J. T. said, looking at me as he slammed out of the studio.

Pippa stopped fiddling with her shoe and put her foot back down. She lit up like she was glad to see me and like she hadn't been about to throw the shoes off her feet at J. T.

"You told him what I said about the song sounding like someone else's?" I asked.

"No, I told him I wanted to use your song."

"What are you talking about?" I asked, alarm bells going off somewhere in my head.

"The song you sent me last night."

"I didn't send anything."

She pulled out her phone, which was blinged out in pink rhinestones—or at least I hoped they were rhinestones. Otherwise that phone probably cost more than Mom made at work for a year at the hospital.

"How did you get this?" I asked, looking at myself on-screen. I was singing my favorite of my own songs, "Alone with Me."

"Someone sent it to me. I just assumed it was you." She said it like it was no big deal.

"It wasn't." Another thought hit me. "Oh no, if J. T. finds out and thinks I did . . ."

She showed me the text. The number looked familiar. I pulled out my own phone. It matched James's number, except for the last digit. Could it be Harmon Holt's number?

"I'll tell J. T. I found it myself. You're missing the point. I loved your song, and I want to use it on my album. With a few tweaks, of course. But we can work those out together."

My head was spinning. Pippa wanted to sing my song, and she wanted me to help her "tweak it."

"The point is that I love it. It's perfect. It's new. It says all the stuff I've been feeling about being alone in a school full of people. Okay, not school, but you know what I mean. You get what it's like. I love it. And we are going to make such beautiful music together." Pippa gave me a crushing hug.

# SIXTEEN

The surprises kept on coming. Malik was waiting for me when I got back from seeing Pippa. He was sitting at his desk, tapping away on his tablet.

"You won't believe what just happened," I said, sitting down at my intern desk opposite him.

"Me first," Malik said, seeming a little nervous.

"Am I fired? I'm totally fired, aren't I?" Maybe it would be a relief to have all this be over. But even though everything was kind of screwed up, I wasn't ready to leave yet.

"You're not fired."

But something had to be wrong.

He paced away from me.

"J. T. left for the day. He'll cool off. Once he fired me in the morning because he was sure that I was secretly giving him decaf. And then he called me back two hours later and rehired me because he couldn't find any of his files."

"So I'm not fired? So what is it?"

"I've been thinking about this a lot since I heard you sing. . . . I want to represent you." Malik blurted suddenly, running his hand over his close-cropped hair.

"You what?"

"I have been working for J. T. for five years, and he thinks he's ready for me to sign someone of my own. And I pick you."

"But me? J. T. hates me."

"J. T. doesn't hate you. He just doesn't get you. But I do. I think you're exactly what the label needs."

I looked at him to see if he was kidding. But Malik didn't kid. He was serious about me.

"Me?" I repeated. "I can't even stand on a stage for longer than five seconds."

"I can help you get over the stage-fright thing. What I can't do is find someone who sings or writes as well as you do, Beth. I watched all your YouTube clips. I heard you sing in the studio the other day. You've got it. You're the real thing."

I didn't know what to say.

"We'd start small—you can keep writing songs for other people. Once the world hears the song you wrote for Pippa, I think I can line up a few other artists you can write for. And when you have a few more singles out there, we can pick one of your songs for you to sing yourself. What do you say?"

"That you're crazy, and J. T. will never go for it!"

"Let me worry about J. T. Now is that a yes?"

"Yes!" I blurted and gave him a hug.

# SEVENTEEN

The next morning I was supposed to see J. T. first thing.

Malik patted me on the shoulder on the way in.

J. T. seemed way calmer than he was yesterday.

"I discussed it with Pippa. We agree that your song has merit."

Had he really changed his mind?

"But it needs a lot of work. I need it to be more upbeat and commercial. The way it is now, it's sad and it has no romance. Her fans will never go for that."

I went for broke. "I'm one of her fans, and I would totally go for it. That's what makes it special. It's about her being like every other girl, feeling a little lonely even when she's surrounded. Everyone feels that way sometimes, even Pippa."

"It's a downer. And Pippa's fans might be living small, pathetic lives, but they don't want to know that Pippa is just like them. They want to think that she's better than they are. That she doesn't have a miserable moment in her life. That if they listen to her they might be a little more like her. A little happier, a little more glamorous. That's her brand. That's what's made us millions and millions of dollars, and that's why we're not changing that now, do you understand?"

"Yes, but . . ." My mind was reeling. But I understood what he wanted. What he was asking.

"No buts. If you make the changes I request, there's an opportunity here for you."

"What are you talking about?"

"If Pippa sings your song, after we make the changes, then I will include it on her new album, and you will get a songwriting credit and be paid for your services."

I rocked back on my flats. J. T. Lane wanted to buy my song. He wanted to change everything about it. But he still wanted to buy it.

"Do exactly what I say, and you'll be in the liner notes. Don't, and I'll send you on the first bus back to Nowheresville."

When I exited the office, I filled Malik in about everything.

"That's amazing."

Malik was thrilled. This was better than he'd even imagined it. But something nagged at me. I didn't know how I could do what he wanted me to do—to change the song into something it wasn't.

# EIGHTEEN

I showed up at the Plaza Hotel, notebook in hand, feeling really stupid and really excited at the exact same moment. Pippa's assistant opened the door to her suite. The assistant always looked like she was completely on edge, ready to pounce at Pippa's next request. Whatever it was.

Pippa, no makeup, hair still wet, sat cross-legged on the big tufted sofa in the center of the room. Gone were the wig, the heels, and all the things that made her larger than life. She looked smaller, realer. I liked her like this. But

I wasn't 100 percent sure I knew how to talk to this Pippa either.

"How does this work?" I asked. This was the first time I'd ever written a song with someone, the first time I'd hung out with a rock star.

She grabbed a pink guitar out of a covered case on the floor next to her. The guitar itself wasn't the one I'd seen her use on stage. This one was old and beat-up, like the one I had back home. Maybe it was her first guitar, too.

"I got room service—if this isn't good for you, then I can have room service send some more up. I'm on a diet. I'm always on a diet, but I can't write without food. You?"

"I like food . . . I mean, I'm not on a diet." I blurted. "Um I mean, it looks great."

"This is not going to work," she announced suddenly, putting the guitar back down in its case.

"Okay, I can go . . ." I said. I could feel the blood rushing to my face.

"No, I mean, if this is going to work, you have to stop thinking of me as Pippa, recording star. You have to think of me as Pippa, just another girl who writes songs like you."

I sat back down, relieved. But it was way easier said than done.

"But you are Pippa. And I'm . . ."

"Don't finish that thought. Anyone who works with me is Pippa-fied."

I burst out laughing.

"What? Gaga has her monsters. Mariah has her lambs. I have the Pips."

I laughed harder.

I eyed the phone next to her guitar, a little concerned that she might throw it in my direction. But instead she deadpanned, "I have to work on my catchphrases." And then she began laughing, too.

'Yes, you do," I said. And we were off.

# NINETEEN

"How do you write a song?" she asked, genuinely curious, a few hours into our session.

I still couldn't get over Pippa asking me for advice.

"I don't know. It just kind of comes to me," I said. "I guess, I just draw from the stuff that's around me. And the stuff that I wish that was."

Her life was so big. So glamorous. I'd think that she would have so much more to write about. I was glad that she was doing the strumming. I knew a little piano and guitar. I'd saved up and bought a guitar last Christmas. But I hadn't had lessons. I was getting better, but I didn't want to play in front of her. I looked down at my hands holding a croissant. I could see that they were still a little shaky and sweaty,

"How do you?" I parroted back.

"I've never really done it on my own—someone else just writes it, and then I tell them what I want to change."

"But your name is on everything!" I blurted. This wasn't Coco-water. This was her music. Wasn't it supposed to be somehow about her?

"It's the only way I can get a piece of the royalties—"

"And you're okay with that?"

"Besides, J. T. says I don't actually make my own perfume, I just tell them what I'd like it to smell like—but it's my name that sells the song, so . . ."

"Right, of course. I have so much to learn about this business," I said, half-expecting a phone to come flying at my head. I pulled myself together, reminding myself that I had a job to do, and to not be so judgy.

"So do you just want me to write it for you?"

I picked up the notebook, feeling a little like I was lending my homework to someone who hadn't done any of the work.

Pippa shook her head. "I'm not okay with it. I want this album to be different. I want a little piece of me to be in this song. Okay, a lot of me. I want the real Pippa to just stand up—like you said."

"And you want me to help you? This is crazy. I'm just . . . an intern."

"No, you're a songwriter."

She said it with such certainty that I almost believed her. Or maybe I just really, really wanted to.

# TWENTY

When I left we arranged to meet the next night after I finished at the office.

"Musicians have a lot in common with vampires. They start late, wear sunglasses at night, and seem to rely on a pretty rare commodity to survive. Not blood. fame," she joked.

I hadn't managed to make any of the changes that J. T. wanted. The song seemed to have a life of its own. Like it knew exactly what it wanted to do and say. And Pippa and I, even though we were from completely different worlds, were on completely the same page.

The next night we started again.

When we took a food break, I asked, "So what does it feel like?"

"What?"

"Being in front of all those people? I can't imagine it."

She paused like she was thinking about it, then said, "It's terrifying. It's like looking out into a sea of people. But it's a rush—you feel like you want to run for like a second, and then you feel this energy coming back from the crowd. It's like pure love—or adoration or something. I know it sounds stupid, but there's nothing like it. It's like, you write this song in your room and it's all yours, but when you're on stage you realize it doesn't just belong to you anymore. It kind of has become something bigger. It belongs to all of them, too. And it's kind of amazing. I sound like an idiot, don't I."

"No, you sound like someone who loves what you do. I still don't think I could ever do it."

"Look, I'm thrilled to take your gorgeous songs as long as you are giving them away. But one day that big voice of yours is going to want to get out, and it's going to be amazing."

I shook my head and said, "No way."

But I was saying it to Pippa. My songwriting partner. Some small part of me wondered: if I could do this, what else could I do?

# TWENTY-ONE

"You broke my star. I expect you to fix her," J. T. said, leaning back in his chair. He was staring at the memory card that I had brought in from the last night's session with Pippa.

"She's a person. I can't just change her mind. She's pretty certain about the direction she wants to go in." I pointed at the memory card. "If you just listen. Then maybe."

"I don't need to listen. I need you to fix her." He repeated it like she was a thing and not a person.

"You did it once. Do it again. You put all that crap in her head. About honesty and being the real her. The world loves the fake her. The real her will never sell. The real her is a boring little brat with nothing to say."

Did Pippa know that J. T. talked about her like that? I knew now more than ever that the music business was a business. But wasn't there room for Pippa to grow in it?

I gulped hard. Trying to think of the right thing to say. Knowing that the more that I talked, the angrier he seemed to get.

"You ever watch those animal shows on the Animal Channel?"

"No?" I said, not sure where this was going.

"Well, they have a show that's all about babies that have lost their moms and end up mistaking some other creature for their parent. Like dogs raising baby lions or cats raising baby chicks. The thing is, Pippa is kind of like that."

"A baby lion?"

"She's spent the last three years following all my advice. Now, for some reason, she's following yours. I just need you to lead her in the right direction. And if you don't, you can kiss your deal here goodbye."

On the desk there was a really official-looking contract with my name on it.

I thought of all the arguments against picking it up—my pride, Pippa's trust—but the arguments for it won out. Money for school. Money for Mom. Maybe even a future in this business. It was just one song, right? I could do this.

He pushed it in my direction. I picked it up and headed out of the office.

# TWENTY-TWO

I met Paloma for dinner. She was chattering on and on about another successful day at the fashion mag. She seemd to have it all figured out, while I was screwing up on a daily basis. She saw my work drama differently than I did.

"You're kidding, right? Your first week totally beat my first week. You are practically BFFs with an icon."

I didn't know if Pippa qualified as an icon, and we certainly weren't BFFs. but it was good talking to Paloma. She was totally wrong, but at least she was on my side.

I hadn't told my mom about the possibility of the song yet. She would have told me not to dream too big. I wanted to hold onto dreaming at least a little while longer. I put the contract in an envelope for her, but I couldn't bring myself to send it. (I was still a minor, so of course my mom had to sign it too.)

I texted Mercedes about everything. She loved Pippa too. But she loved me more.

Her text read:

*Take the contract, Pippa can find her artistic freedom after you have a record deal. Don't overthink.*

# TWENTY-THREE

The next night Pippa wanted to work at the restaurant in her hotel. When I arrived I was stunned to find that no one else was there. She'd rented the whole place out. When I got to the café, Pippa walked in, smiling broadly. She looked excited. "So I made some changes. I worked on the bridge. I think you'll like it. But if you don't, we can change it back."

She looked so incredibly excited about the song. She handed me some sheet music with our new lyrics written on it. I felt even worse about trying to change it back.

I reminded myself that I didn't owe Pippa anything. So what if she didn't have complete artistic freedom? She had millions of fans and millions of dollars to help her get over it.

"Listen." She began strumming the guitar and singing my song.

And it did sound good. It was complicated and beautiful and it left me speechless. Could I really try and undo that? It didn't feel right.

"I think it's great," I said with a smile that I didn't feel. "But maybe we should try it another way. Just to see what else we like."

Pippa's face shifted with confusion—then she brightened.

"Sure, if you think so. I thought we had it down. But I trust you completely."

I felt the word *trust* hit me somewhere in my chest. She trusted me. And right now, I wasn't entirely sure she should have.

# TWENTY-FOUR

The next morning, after an almost all-nighter with Pippa, I went to see J. T. with a copy of the song that we had now rewritten to his specifications. I felt sick looking at all the changes. J. T. was wearing a half-finished blue suit, and an old man was circling him, holding a fistful of pins. J. T. was getting fitted for the Blue Party. The proceeds of the party would go to music education. Pippa would debut her latest track there.

"Harmon's one of our biggest donors," J. T. said.

I wondered if he'd actually be there.

Malik looked at my face as if he could read what I was thinking. "Harmon's checks always show, but he never does."

"Oh, too bad."

I didn't know what I would say to the mysterious Harmon Holt, who had changed my life. "Thank you" didn't seem big enough. I tuned back to J. T., who was looking at me again.

"Did you do it? Is she ready?" he demanded, now studying the seams of his shiny blue jacket.

"She's on board with the direction you asked for," I said, feeling super guilty.

"Good girl," he said. His smile made me feel that much worse.

# TWENTY-FIVE

"Close," Paloma demanded. But I kept my eyes open and shook my head when she picked up a little pot of blue eye shadow. I wasn't wearing that.

She was giving me a mini makeover with the free makeup she'd gotten from "The Closet" at her magazine gig.

"Trust me," she said.

I nodded, but my mind went back to Pippa and the song. "Pippa trusted me, and I totally lied to her," I blurted.

"You can't make an enemy of J. T. Lane. He's

like a god in the music industry. That would be like me crossing Anna Wintour."

I blinked up at her. "Who's that?"

"She's like the goddess of fashion. Everyone who's anyone listens to her. And if you don't, you're no one. It sounds like J. T. holds the same place in the music world. You don't want to be no one, do you?"

"But the song . . ."

"It's one song. When you're big and famous, you can write what you want. But this is your ticket. This could be your first shot. So suck it up and do it the way that he wants. People would kill for a chance like this. Don't blow it."

"But what about what Pippa wants? She's already big and famous, and she's still not doing what she wants."

She shrugged, not having an answer for that.

She held up the little pot of blue shadow again.

I closed my eyes, giving in to her choice for me. But was I going to give in to J. T.'s?

# TWENTY-SIX

The party was big. And loud. I didn't have anything blue, so Pippa insisted on loaning me something. It was shorter and sparklier than anything I would have picked out for myself ever. But it was blue.

There was a swimming pool in the middle of the room with candles and blue lanterns floating on its surface. It was pretty.

There was a stage set up at the other end of the room.

I found Pippa in the room behind it, putting the finishing touches on her blue mermaid costume. The stage was going to float over the pool in the middle of the number. She looked amazing. Ridiculous, but amazing. So much for our simple real-girl song. My song was going to be a full-on spectacle, complete with dancers and a fill orchestra.

"You look so beautiful," I said.

"You too. The dress suits you. Now if you'd only try one of my wigs . . ." I patted down my own blunt cut. I liked still looking a little like me.

She frowned at herself in the full-length mirror of her dressing room. "You sure it's not too much? It's a long way from what we started with."

I smiled back, almost tearing up. "It's great. You're still you, Pippa. Only Pippa-fied." She laughed and tried to move her tail.

"It's funny, I'm never nervous. But I'm nervous now. It feels good to be nervous, you know?" Pippa said, looking out at the crowd.

"I'm always nervous."

"You shouldn't be. You're not the one who's going to be singing."

She started doing her vocal exercises, stretching out her mouth and making clucking noises. She waved me away as if she needed privacy.

When I walked back out into the party, I saw someone I wasn't expecting.

It was James, Harmon Holt's assistant, in the flesh, standing near the stage.

"What are you doing here?" I asked.

"Since I missed our meet-and-greet, I thought I'd drop in and drop Harmon's check off in person."

"Is he here?" I asked, scanning the crowd.

He shook his head.

"I still can't believe I'm here," I said.

"Well, I hear that you're doing amazing. A songwriting credit? I know I'm not supposed to say this, but that's probably one for the record books. And our interns have done some pretty amazing things. Just between you and me, this puts you in really good standing for a scholarship. You know Mr. Holt likes to grant those too, right?"

I couldn't breathe for second. I was maybe getting even further rewarded for doing the wrong thing.

"You okay?"

"I'm great," I said, but my voice sounded shaky.

"You look a little green," he assessed.

"I'm fine. It's just a lot to take in."

"Well, keep up the good work. I'll see you at the after-party." He squeezed my hand and began to move off.

"James?" I stopped him.

"Yes?" He turned around, his incredibly pretty profile turning back to me.

"What does Harmon Holt think about . . . compromise in business? You, know to get what you really want."

James paused, as if he was thinking of the right thing to say—or at least what his boss would say. "Good question. I guess Harmon would say that compromise can be a good thing, a necessary thing, just so long you don't compromise yourself."

With that he disappeared into the crowd.

# TWENTY-SEVEN

When I got to the dressing room, she wasn't there, but Malik was.

"Where is she?" I asked Malik.

"She's in the bathroom. I was checking on her. What are you doing?" he asked, frowning a little like he could read what I was about to do.

"Remember how you said that you were looking for someone who had something to say? How that's what you thought the music world was missing? Well, if you believe that, we can't stop Pippa from saying what she wants to say, can we?"

I knew it wasn't just my career on the line. It was Malik's, too. I had to get to her before the show started. But I needed his permission first. He nodded understanding and stepped back out into the party.

A few seconds later, Pippa waddled into the dressing room with the aid of her assistant. She waved her away.

"Remind me to give her a bonus for that." She laughed at her own joke and then trained her brown eyes on me. "What is it?" She smiled up at me. Her white chiffon dress draped across one shoulder. "What do you think?"

She was asking about the outfit, but I was thinking about the song. "I think you should sing it the original way. The way we wrote it."

Her pretty face looked confused. "You said this version was better."

"Do you think it's better?" I asked, meeting her eyes.

"No, but you said . . ."

"There's no point doing it unless *you're* loving it, right?"

"Pippa-fied," she said with a smile.

# TWENTY-EIGHT

Fifteen minutes later, Pippa reemerged from her dressing room dressed as herself. Not in the mermaid costume. Not in her wig. No heels. No tail in sight. No orchestra. No dancers. She was wearing a white slip that skimmed her thin, long body, and she was holding her guitar—the beat-up one, not the bedazzled one that she usully used. She stepped onto the stage.

The crowd gasped, and so did I. James was about to exit, but he paused at the door and smiled at me.

Just then the real Pippa began to sing. Pippa

stood onstage and sang the song our way.

*I know all the faces in the room*
*They're expecting the same old tune.*
*They think they know me, too,*
*They've seen all my moves, they've heard it*
*all before.*
*But they don't know the real me.*
*It's not their fault they've only seen the me*
*that I want them to see.*

Her voice filled the room. And the reaction was mixed. Some people fell instantly in love with it—other people looked a little confused. J. T. looked downright mad.

Pippa looked happy, like she was completely unaware of the mixed reaction of the crowd. When she finished the song, she launched into a compilation of her old hits. The crowd was completely with her this time.

I listened to Malik and J. T. and the other execs talking a few paces away.

"It's fine. We can contain it," one of the other suits said.

J. T. shook his head.

"Did we take everyone's cell phone before we started this thing?"

Malik shook his head. "We'd lose half the crowd before they would give up their iPhones."

"Then there's no way that it isn't posted right now," said J. T.

I pulled out my phone and did a search. J. T. was right. It was all over the Web. Now we just had to wait and see what the rest of the world thought of the new Pippa.

J. T. pulled Malik over to the bar. I couldn't hear them, but J. T. was pointing at Malik, and it didn't look like he was accusing him of getting decaf. I started looking up bus fares on my phone.

# TWENTY-NINE

Malik finally broke free and found me.

"So I'm fired, right?" I asked for probably the third time since I got to Bonified.

"No, J. T. wants you to stay," he said, but he didn't give me his usual, it-will-all-be-okay expression. He looked worried. He had tied himself to me when he asked to sign me. I hoped that when I dropped like a stone, I wouldn't drag him down and out with me.

"Why? I screwed everything up."

"Pippa likes you. He wants you to see this through with her."

"But why?"

"He's giving you the opportunity to fix this," he said quietly.

"He still wants me to change her mind."

He nodded. "But he's taking steps to stop it himself."

# THIRTY

The next day, J. T. was talking to Pippa in a really quiet, really nice voice. The kind he only used with talent, and that he never used with me. We were all back at Bonified's offices after the after-party. "So you gave it a shot. You tried your own way. It clearly didn't work. And that's fine. We just give them more of what they want, and it will all be forgotten."

J. T. was holding a blog post about last night's performance. The headline was "Pippa Misfires: Teen Dream Turns in Nightmare Performance at Blue Party."

Pippa pushed the iPad aside. Was she in denial, or did she just not care? My own heart sank for her and for myself. So much for college money or hearing my song on the radio or seeing the look on Michelle's face at school when she found out about it.

"What if I don't want to forget?" Pippa said quietly.

"Excuse me?" J. T. demanded, a look of confusion replacing his usual smirk.

"I liked singing that song. I had more fun up there than I've had in years. And I want to do it again. And again. My fans might not have been with me, but they just need a minute to catch up. And when they do, they will love it, like they always have."

J. T. shook his head.

"This is your career, Pippa. You only have a minute. And if you disappoint them now, they will be on to the next thing. You have a tiny window of being this hot. And you cannot let it pass. You have to make all that you can while you can."

She looked at me to back her up.

But I didn't say anything. Then J. T. nailed me with a look.

I croaked, "I don't want you to lose what you have. I know how hard you worked to get there. I can't take that kind of responsibility. I would never forgive myself."

Pippa's eyes flashed with anger and then softened with hurt. "You don't have faith in me either."

"It's not that," I protested. But it was too late.

"Either you do or you don't," she said.

"You have so much at stake." I could feel tears prickling, but I willed them to stop. I wouldn't cry in front of J. T.

Pippa, looking more hurt than I thought she was capable of being, didn't throw a tantrum. She got quiet. Really quiet. She picked up her phone and walked out of the room.

J. T. nodded at me once and followed her out.

# THIRTY-ONE

The next day was just weird. I made copies and got coffee, but all I wanted to do was scream. I was on the verge of doing it when Malik found me.

"Follow me. You need to see this." He pulled me out of the copy room. "J. T. cherry-picked that bad blog review. I have a feeling it's about to backfire." He led me into a big conference room filled with guys in suits.

"Lawyers? Execs?" I asked, sliding into a seat next to Malik's—away from the table.

Malik whispered, "Both. The guy with the ugly goatee is J. T.'s boss."

Pippa sat at the head of the table. She blinked her superlong lashes in every direction. She didn't look intimidated. But I was.

"Since you weren't inclined to listen to me, I thought you might listen to your contract."

Pippa looked across at J. T., her face still unreadable.

"We can't release this single. It goes against your brand. And we only want the best for you." J. T. sounded bored.

Pippa continued. "The contract states that if I can demonstrate that the new material would boost my brand, then I, the artist, have the right to go forward with material of my own creation."

J. T. stared at me as if asking whether I'd had anything to do with Pippa knowing what was in her contract.

I nudged Malik. He kept staring straight ahead, but the tiniest smile played on his full lips.

"Here you go. The hashtag is *newpippa*." She pulled out her cell phone and began reading from Twitter.

"I love the new song. Where can I get it."

"If this is what the rest of the album is like, I can't wait to buy it."

"Just when I thought that Pippa couldn't get any better, she does this. Can't wait to buy the new song."

J. T. sneered, "You can't seriously be using Twitter as proof."

"You use it all the time. Aren't you the one who's always talking about my social media index? And I'd say that this song brings it way up."

Several of the suits were deep in their own phones.

One said, "#newpippa's trending."

"A million tweets and counting," added a guy with a ponytail.

"J. T., we share your concerns about the new material," said one of the execs. Pippa's face fell, and a twinkle of anger flashed in her golden-brown eyes. "However, she's right. J. T., you've spent the better part of two years showing us how social media numbers are a good indicator of future sales." He turned to Pippa. "Don't let us down."

With that, the room cleared. J. T. was clearly pissed, but he didn't say another word. I never thought of J. T. answering to anybody. But I guess everyone answered to someone—except maybe Harmon Holt.

Pippa broke into a huge smile and gave me a hug.

"Pippa, that was amazing. You were so brilliant," I squealed.

"I was, wasn't I? But I couldn't have done it without this guy. Thank you," she mouthed to Malik.

"I don't know what you're talking about." He shrugged and smiled.

She winked at him. "J. T. would kill whoever sent Pippa a copy of her contract with certain portions highlighted."

And for the first time I met him, he was speechless.

Pippa laughed and linked her arm through mine. "We have to hurry."

"What for?"

"We have a press conference."

# THIRTY-TWO

A few minutes later we were standing in front of the press on Bonified's in-house stage. Just before she walked on stage, Pippa grabbed my hand and informed me that she expected me to sing backup for her. I shook my head. I looked out into the sea of press that had filled the small auditorium on the fifth floor.

"You can do this. I've heard your voice. It's almost as good as mine." She laughed when she said it. "You know what I do when I'm singing. I pick someone in the crowd and sing to them so that it isn't so overwhelming."

"You mean someone in your entourage."

"Sometimes. But I like picking someone I don't know. The important thing is that you make it so that it's just you and the other person. Then it isn't so scary." She walked out, and the press began yelling questions. "I'll answer all your questions. But first, a song."

Malik was standing beside me. He looked at me a long beat and then nodded.

Pippa continued. "None of this would have been possible without the songwriter, Beth Thorne."

I tried to take a step back into the crowd, but Malik pushed me forward.

The spotlight found me.

I waved at the crowd.

"Beth is going to come up here and join me."

I shook my head.

"Come on, Beth. Crowd, help me out here. Don't we want Beth? Beth! Beth! Beth!!"

She could scream anything and they would repeat it. But they were screaming my name.

Malik pushed me forward again, toward the stage. He looked at me. "You can do this," he said.

Malik had faith in me, and so did Pippa. I didn't even bother looking for J. T. in the crowd. If I did, I would run out of the club.

I took the stage and began to sing.

# THIRTY-THREE

*Dear Mr. Holt,*

*Music was my secret. Thank you for bringing it out into the light. I never thought I could be a singer/songwriter. But this summer proved to me that I could do a lot of things I never thought I could. Singing in front of a crowd, standing up for my lyrics. I did that, but only because you gave me the opportunity.*

*I understand how difficult the business is now, and I know I have a very long way to go. But now I have the tools to try.*

*Sincerely,*
*Beth Thorne*

## ABOUT THE AUTHOR

D. M. Paige attended Columbia University and her first internship eventually led her to her first writing job at *Guiding Light*, a soap opera. She writes and lives in New York City.

# IT'S THE OPPORTUNITY OF A LIFETIME— IF YOU CAN HANDLE IT.

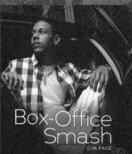

Box-Office Smash
D.M. PAIGE

THE OPPORTUNITY

The Campaign
ELIZABETH KARRE

THE OPPORTUNITY

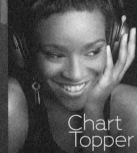

Chart Topper
D.M. PAIGE

THE OPPORTUNITY

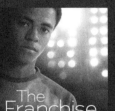

The Franchise
PATRICK JONES with BRENT CHARTIER

THE OPPORTUNITY

Going to Press
D.M. PAIGE

THE OPPORTUNITY

Size 0
D.M. PAIGE

THE OPPORTUNITY

# THE OPPORTUNITY